leonard oprea

THEOPHIL MAGUS IN BATON ROUGE

a haiku novel

2007

LEONARD OPREA (**b.** December 1953) **is a contemporary** *Romanian* **writer.**

He was born in Prejmer, a village in Braşov (Kronstadt) County in the eastern part of Transylvania, central Romania. A graduate of the University of Braşov, he specialized in mass-media communication at the University of California at Chico in 1990.

Since 1999 he has been living in the USA, currently in Boston, Massachusetts.

Leonard Oprea was an anti-communist dissident in Romania during Ceausescu's dictatorship. Between 1980 and 1987 he published one book and some short stories in the most important literary reviews and won many national literary prizes. After 1987 the *Securitate*, the secret police of the Communist regime, officially forbade the publication of his writings, considering them subversive.

After the Romanian Revolution of 1989, living in Bucharest, he became a well-known Romanian writer, journalist and editor. He was able to resume publishing his works: novels, short stories, tales and essays, meditations etc. He founded the Romanian Publishing House *Athena*, the *Vladimir Colin* Romanian Cultural Foundation as well as the *Vladimir Colin* international awards.

Links:

http://en.wikipedia.org/wiki/Leonard_Oprea, www.google.com, www. amazon.com, www.barnes&noble.com

Works:

- *Domenii interzise* (Forbidden areas) - short stories and novellas; Albatros Publishing House - 1984, Romania.

- *Radiografia clipei* (The x-ray of an instant) - short stories and novellas forbidden by the Romanian Communist dictatorship in 1987; Dacia Publishing House - 1990, Romania; the second edition with critical references at Curtea Veche Publishing - 2003,

Romania; electronic book by "LiterNet" www.liternet.ro/, 2005, Romania.

- *Cămaşa de forţă* (The Straitjacket) a novel banned by the Romanian Communist dictatorship in 1988; Nemira Publishing House - 1992, Romania; the second edition with critical references at Curtea Veche Publishing - 2004, Romania; electronic book by "LiterNet" www.liternet.ro/, 2005, Romania.

- The Trilogy of Theophil Magus:

  o *Cele Nouă Invăţături ale lui Theophil Magus despre Magia Transilvană* (The Nine Teachings of Theophil Magus on Transylvanian Magic) - Polirom Publishing House - 2000, Romania; electronic book by "LiterNet" www.liternet.ro/, 2003, Romania.

  o The Book Of Theophil Magus Or 40 Tales About Man (Cartea lui Theophil Magus sau 40 de Poveşti despre Om) - Polirom Publishing House - 2001, Romania. *English version*, October 2003, edited in the USA by Ingram Book Group/ 1stBooks Library; new edition by AuthorHouse - 2004, USA.

  o *Meditaţiile lui Theophil Magus sau Simple Cugetări Creştine la Începutul Mileniului III* (The Meditations of Theophil Magus or Simple Christian Thoughts at the Beginning of the Third Millennium) - Polirom Publishing House - 2002, Romania; electronic book by "LiterNet" www.liternet.ro/, 2004, Romania.

- Theophil Magus - Confessions 2004-2006 ("Universal Dalsi" Publishing House, 2007, Romania)

Quotations about *Leonard Oprea*'s work:

The Book of Theophil Magus or 40 Tales about Man is situated in the strange no man's land where everyday life becomes truly magical. I consider these writings as splendid expressions of a unique vision of our fragmented but marvelously exciting world. *Leonard Oprea*'s style combines a discovery of hidden meanings of words with a fabulous sense of secret humor. His works received the highest praises from the most influential critics, who rightly compared his vision to works by Thomas Mann, Borges or Paulo Coelho. (*Vladimir Tismăneanu* - philosopher, author, essayist and editor; backcover of *The Book of Theophil Magus or 40 Tales about Man*, AuthorHouse - 2003, USA)

In The Book of Theophil Magus a great variety of sacred and profane themes, archaic, mythical, contemporary (*Moses, Gandhi, Christmas, children, journalism, pilgrimage* etc.) serves as vivid stimulation for this literary adventure, written with humor, knowledge and wit . . . in an inviting dialogue with the reader. (*Norman Manea* - author and essayist; backcover of *The Book of Theophil Magus or 40 Tales about Man*, AuthorHouse - 2003, USA)

Leonard Oprea's 40 Tales about Man range from the depiction of the everyday to the mythological and Borgesian to the religious. Honored with numbers of prizes in his native Romania, this writer is a true iconoclast and a true talent. (*Adam Sorkin* - author, essayist and editor; backcover of *The Book of Theophil Magus or 40 Tales about Man*, AuthorHouse - 2003, USA)

In Romania, *Leonard Oprea* is a distinguished writer. His fiction and non-fiction work was censored during the Communist dictatorship. In my opinion, here in the USA, *Leonard Oprea* could make a genuine contribution to our current writing landscape. (*Andrei Codrescu* - poet, author, NPR commentator, essayist; from amazon.com review of *The Book of Theophil Magus or 40 Tales about Man*, AuthorHouse - 2003, USA)

Leonard Oprea

THEOPHIL MAGUS
IN
BATON ROUGE

A NOVEL

in

101 AMERICAN HAIKU

***

Edition revised by _Bogdan Stefanescu_

Library of Congress Control Number: 2007909824
ISBN: Hardcover 978-1-4363-0966-0
Softcover 978-1-4363-0965-3

***
Front cover - "Christ as Man of Sorrow" by Albrecht Durer /about 1494-1495/ Oil
on panel, 30 x 19 cm
***
Interior illustrations - engravings by Albrecht Durer (1471-1528)
***
Interior photos by Leonard Oprea
***
Editorial Adviser: Frieda Lovett
***

This book was printed in the United States of America.

To order additional copies of this book, contact:
Xlibris Corporation
1-888-795-4274
www.Xlibris.com
Orders@Xlibris.com
45636

CONTENTS

I dedicate this haiku novel to:

Anna-Maria, Brigitte, Saint Leonard of Port Maurice and Ara.

***

This is not a poetry book.
This is not a Haiku book.
This is a book about real life.
My life in Baton Rouge, Louisiana.
This book is a novel.
A HAIKU NOVEL.
PROBABLY THE FIRST HAIKU NOVEL WORLDWIDE.
And because it is time to let your imagination free, my friends,
I give you 101 American Haiku and a Haiku Epilogue to start with.
Enjoy!

LEONARD'S GIANT LEAP OF FANCY

by *Bogdan Stefanescu*

First, there's no such thing as a haiku novel. At least, not until you've read this book. Not until Leonard Oprea thought it could exist. How did it suddenly become possible? How can anyone imagine that the shortest text in the lyrical tradition may be aggregated into the longest form of epic prose?

Also, there's no such thing as a haiku psalm to the Christian God of Love. How can anyone think of hailing Jesus in a Japanese poem?

Nor was there such a thing as democracy in Romania for half a century. Before the 1989 anti-communist uprising, a free life was simply unthinkable - we had been born, raised, wedded, and multiplied under tyranny. And yet, in Leonard Oprea's mind freedom was a real thing, not just a shy phantom of our secret dreamworld.

And even after communism crumbled, there could be no realistic talk of Leonard Oprea the American writer; the man spoke no English before he moved to the United States seven years later. How can he be writing innovative books in English after only a few years? And why doesn't his occasionally Chinese-sounding syntax crumble, too, how does it miraculously take wing?

How? How does he do all these things? If you ask me, it probably takes a demented leap of fancy to bridge the solid world of being with the invisible realm of the not-there-yet.

No, not faith, fancy. Faith is blind, it takes truths like God, or good for granted, it relies on their already being there for us. Fancy creates something that hasn't been there from the start. New beings, new worlds, new truths pop out of nowhere, materializing like unexpected gifts. The once impossible is now only natural.

*　　*　　*

A haiku novel, I've just found, is easy to read, but difficult to understand. You can read one page at a time and a page is a mere 17 syllables. The sentences are short, the words - simple. You don't have to remember dozens of names or incidents in order to go along with the reading. You can simply concentrate on the page in front of you.

But that is never enough to understand it all. Many times you will find that each individual haiku, while seemingly unpretentious, is, in fact, elliptical and esoteric. You need to ponder and explore it with your imaginative hearts to find its possible meanings. (Yes, more than one in most cases.) Once you have settled for its provisional significance, you take the next step and look for the hidden links between the haiku episodes. Sometimes the links join neighboring poems, sometimes they span several pages. The haikus may be linked in pairs or in clusters. Dare one ever hope to find the miraculous key to bringing them all together?

I suggest you start with this exercise: read one page in the morning and repeat the poem as many times as you can throughout the day, until it becomes familiar, then strange, outlandish. Once it is securely lodged in your memory it will start to work its way into your heart and wit. Be sure to repeat your little mantra of the day in the quieter hours of the evening and as you lay in your bed, ready to sleep. As the magic words resound peacefully in your head, the poem will envelop you in its grace and shield you from the noise and worries. It will also open up the door to another world, making you feel once again like an excited child hiding in the small storeroom with a flashlight, looking at things he didn't even know existed. In that "small" space, you'll be taking *a giant leap of fancy*.

(Bogdan Stefanescu - New York, December 3, 2007)

THE TALE OF THE AUTHOR

Dear Reader,

For a writer coming from the paroxysmal post-1989 Eastern Europe, living in Louisiana means sharing in the magical realm of Faulkner and Tennessee Williams, of Andrei Codrescu and New Orleans, Mardi Gras, Bourbon Street, and the French Quarter. Especially if he comes from Bucharest, the Romanian metropolis, once known as "Little Paris".

But he is now in Baton Rouge. And Red Stick, the so called capital of Louisiana, is with all due respect, no more than that "something" elusive which belongs to the world of Citizen Kafka. And this some*thing* "thing" has the ID-papers to prove it.

Imagine this some*thing* neither a village, nor a city, with no sidewalks and no public transport for its more than 500,000 inhabitants, where, no matter how scorching the heat, robots resembling golems run tirelessly around two lakes . . . In which the shrines for daily worship are Wal Mart and the Mall . . . In which downtown is a mere ghost town . . . In which the spoken American English is a swamp dialect. In which the Civil War has not yet been waged . . . In which only the sky, live-oaks, squirrels and birds, lakes and cypresses are . . . human.

How can you tell the story of one year of your life in this simply . . . incredible world?

> *Definitely, neither prose, nor poetry or the essay will do the trick.*
> *Since everything seems to be irreversibly numb, only the flashes of*
> *occasional perceptions can help me to tell you this story.*

15

This is how my **HAIKU NOVEL** in **101 AMERICAN HAIKU** was born. And Basho himself assured me it is as it should be. Taking his advice and allowing myself to be inspired by the master, I wrote the first American novel to consist entirely of haiku. I offer it to you in full confidence.

The Author

THE TALE OF THEOPHIL MAGUS

Baton Rouge is the perfect place where nothing ever happens . . . Nevermore. Red Stick is Kafka's domain - where Kafka would have lasted no more than his condemned protagonist in *The Penal Colony*.

Coming from Bucharest, a metropolis known as the "Little Paris", a Romanian writer arrives in Baton Rouge. But he does not meet with Faulkner or Tennessee Williams in Red Stick, nor does he find Bourbon Street or Mardi Gras or hear the Louisiana blues. All he can hear is the swamp-language of Wal Mart and the malls, and these "temples" are the only places where he can come across its speakers - *golems* for whom the Civil War has not yet taken place. You cannot meet them in the streets for there are no sidewalks. You cannot find them on buses or on the underground for these things do not exist. And only in bars and at football stadiums they make sense to one another. All 500,000 of them.

Naturally, this writer who came to live and work in America now feels like he is going crazy. Then what does he do?! He writes haiku. A haiku may not be told for it is the quintessence of any tale. And the haiku by its very nature is a snapshot of reality itself - no make-up, no fancy clothes, and no witty interpretations. Our man writes haiku about a world that cannot be described any other way. For it is tragic-comically absurd.

Our man writes as he breathes, as he strolls, hears, sees, feels or has sex, as he rejoices or weeps - as he writes. All in admirable and absurd solitude.

His choice: become a "red-sticker" or wander off. America is a great country after all, and it is also known as *The Promised Land*.

17

This is how the story begins:
"... *never ending sky*
a blue note silently plays;
the eagle's lone flight..."

This is how the novel ends:
"... *golden lake at dawn ...*
... thrilled by the eagle's high call -
Lord, thanks: I fly alone!..."

And this is the epilogue:
"... *over the mute lake*
one eagle flies - splinter of ...
haiku diamond..."

Theophil Magus

". . . never ending sky. . .
a blue note silently plays;
the eagle's lone flight. . ."

"... look, one white heron
alights on the magic lake.
I light a candle..."

"... the shining green grass...
my love plays with our puppy;
Lord, I see Your Grace..."

". . . under the live-oak
two squirrels dance like shadows;
that gentle sunrise. . ."

". . . between the bloody swamp
and the purple sky - no hope;
this sunset trapped me. . ."

"... the Old River's blues
is this orange song of sky. . .
Shore at dawn. I breathe. . ."

". . . lonely and sad jazz
of blue trumpet will be on
Bourbon Street my death. . ."

"... cutting in my flesh
sadness smokes my empty soul;
no hope has flowered..."

". . . at nightfall I write;
in daylight I eat and burp.
Bless the rose of life. . ."

"... death reigns on my desk.
Yes, loneliness - kiss my lips!
Lord, that wild lily. . ."

"... see? no fear; look,
rhino's horn is caresses now
the fragile bird's chest..."

".．． my blue heart today
runs and smiles like wild rhinos
on dry earth: for whom?．．."

"... a huge rhino male
tends a small egret female:
I love this Eden. . ."

"... lain down on green grass
I pet my fox terrier.
Simple happiness."

". . . in this sweet-home-cage
I lick the golden bone of. . .
freedom. So, who cares?!. . ."

". . . the shore of steel lake. . .
far-beating bell - my heart; feel?
tremor of water. . ."

". . . there's no way here in
Wal-Mart castle to share your
body and blood like Jesus. . ."

". . . the flaring good light;
no stars no breath - in cold night:
wondering poet. . ."

"... wet windows today;
I feel the fall of big drops:
tasting whiskey-blues..."

"... touched by some nice car,
in twilight a squirrel sleeps;
it looks dead this road. . ."

". . . I'll never forget
the stony silence of trees. . .
the lake's fog. . .And me. . ."

"... good morning sunshine!
I inhale fresh air. Should I
cut my golden strings?..."

"... too many words around...
the bloody camellia flower...
on this ground - my heart..."

"... scarlet sunset could
not thaw these white snow flowers...
magnolia - I dream..."

"... under my shower,
I hear the birds sing at dawn;
thanks God, I'm alive."

"... Chinese food on plate -
amazing oil-painting; I smile;
then, I dare and eat. .."

"... yellow-green light falls;
mad wind snarls in this silence;
hi, storm - I'm alone!..."

". . . the old road's splendor. . .
rose and white flowers' jazz of
the Mardi Gras rain. . ."

"... Hi, sunny Monday!
The church's door. I knock. I read:
'You're loved on Sunday...'"

". . . seated near the Church,
a child stares at the Bank's huge
window - see that, Lord?. . ."

"... April - in Rouge Stick;
the azure over picnickers;
the happy Lent days. . ."

"... heat, dust and big noise:
building site. . .; a few pansies
smile saved by an oak. . ."

". . . the lake; on cypress
this soft landing of dreamy egrets. . .
Christmas of Easter. . ."

"... Mississippi spring.
Silky night - old river tales;
on shore I smoke pipe..."

". . . April morning; man,
there's a cloudy day. . .wind, whispers;
ghosts walk on my street. . ."

". . . at this April's dawn,
a purple haze - on the lake. . .
that silver duck cries. . ."

"... the rainy sunset ending;
on blue lake's mirror I touch
stars of lilac sky. .."

"... leaves gently fall from
the giant live-oak; hear! now
crickets are silent. . ."

"... desolation is
that country railroad station...
only red light sings..."

"... heat at lunch and flies
mesmerized by green lizard. . .
Silence which deafens. . ."

"... ding-dong of all bells...
white magnolias light candles...
Yes, Christ is risen!"

". . . Hi, Christ is risen!
I hail Baton Rouge people. . .
Only "Hi!" comes back. . ."

". . . there is no room here
on highway for peace and faith. . .
A merciless race?!"

"... I see myself here,
on PC, TV dark screens;
shoot the bull's eye - now!"

"... a Cardinal bird
hidden in that green shrub - listen,
a free-heart sings there..."

". . . look! how funny. . .that
yellow kitty hunts butterflies. . .
I love this tiger."

"... light rain over this
quiet Mississippi summer...
Oh, my blue mountains..."

". . . 2 PM and heat
in Baton Rouge; this zombie
smiles sweated: who, me?!. . ."

"... liquid lead - the sky;
liquid lead - the lake; a hope...
this blood-stained sunset?!..."

"... Baton Rouge's blessed lake...
Lord, make me as happy as
a clam at high tide..."

". . . yes, to sleep, to sleep. . .
yes, endless - hopeless dream of
Red Stick's hot summer. . ."

"... Baton Rouge's downtown
on the Memorial Day,
yeah, emptiness' blues. . ."

"... rednecks kick me out
from "Sportsman Paradise"; damn!
I don't have sneakers..."

".. . from nowhere coming,
a swallow flies in my room. . .
no sky - the walls; me. . ."

". . . humid and hot May;
flowered hell of Baton Rouge's
spring. . .empty side-walks. . ."

"... deep sky in the night,
stars, heat - crickets' lamenting:
ordeal of silence..."

". . . the wind died. Stoned lake.
Deadly heat afternoon. . .Yeah,
Red Stick tough men. . .jog. . ."

"... summer days shopping
means I say, yes, Lord, I met
the quick and the dead."

"... night fever lighted by
the lone violin's silky song.
Thank you, nightingale."

"... the wind's dance with
live-oaks and armies of clouds.
Rain, rum - let them come!"

". . . blue and lonesome as
a man can be. . .here in town
crows and I - we are."

". . . in this warm rain shine
golden crown and black sapphires
of sunflowers' fairy. . ."

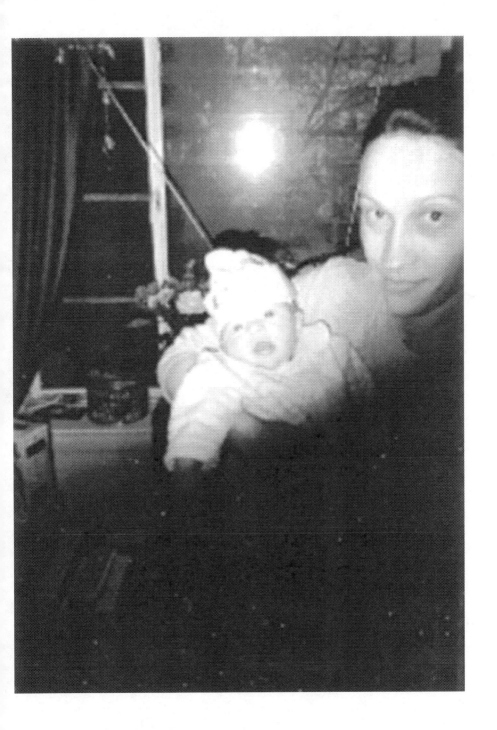

". . . bright red small fish dance
on lake - dragonflies enjoy;
water lily blooms. . ."

". . . the white heron and
a turtle met on a log.
I will miss this lake."

". . . at sunshine my wife,
rocks in live-oak's cradle and
doggy barks - sweet joy. . ."

". . . sunny day, rainy day,
in my neighborhood birds sing.
Beautiful graveyard."

"... one dollar's old face. . .
God's eye: Annuit Coeptis!
Red Stick's Vae Victis!"

"... Saturday morning
jazz & blues on some FM:
Saturday wonder."

"... from the peak of pine
a hawk cries briefly; then flies.
Swamp sunset blues. Hear?"

"... dear mother, I walk.
Only my fox terrier
shadows my shadow."

". . . Red Khmers - Killing Fields. . .
Red Stick - lakes' heavenly lawns. . .
Red Ants - killing kiss. . ."

"... oh! what a misery!
this wild tiger cursed to be
a ball team's mascot..."

". . . silver eye - the moon
lights the lake's quiet slumber:
Sweet dreams, lonely heart!"

". . . happy dwarfs, funny toys
turned to stone by the days' heat. . .
Children's laughs echo. . ."

". . . hiding from the heat
in bushes, those daisies taste
the jokes of an elf. . ."

"... June in Baton Rouge:
torrid torsion of any sense,
torture by torpor..."

"... between boundless blue
and vast green swamp the heat laughs:
only a crow wails..."

"... steamy summer's night seals
the tango which silently
tangles flesh and hearts. .."

". . . today the rain falls
only in Heaven: I burn
in Baton Rouge's hell. . ."

"... fetid scents and whores;
sweaty jazz twist Bourbon Street.
Cajun July 4. . ."

"... there were fireworks.
A few. In Red Stick darkness.
Holy July 4..."

"... White House - a chapel
for Independence Day - blues
of Ray Charles. God smiles. . ."

"... from behind the bars
the cool white tiger eyes me:
hey man, what's wrong there?"

"... these raccoon babies,
the little owl didn't run from
my midnight madness."

"... the flood of sweat's drops
shines all my skins today; see?
sour exquisite corpse..."

". . . morning by morning
I'm viscous inside my brain:
putrid fish on shore. . ."

"... from that young cypress
a white heron calls hoarsely
the wind. Solitude."

"... the heat feeds this city.
Mozart smokes cigars; he's drunk.
The magic flute's death."

"... yesterday I saw
an angel who was lost in
Red Stick. He gave up."

". . . in boiling water
crawfish's rock. . .the good smell of
panic disorder. . ."

"... this grandfather-pine
mates with a burned plot: seeds fly.
Cosmic confetti..."

". . . look at this live-oak:
huge bell tent of Promised Land. . .
here, no man rests here."

"... happy butterfly...
Under trees - a silent flight to
death. Could I practice?"

". . . how are you? I heard.
Well. . ., I say. And I wait. . .What?!
Lord, another ghost?!. . ."

". . . behind that window
of the church a good light prays -
lightning in the night. . ."

"... all the night I walked
with my doggy looking for
fairies - hope is gone..."

"... this summer must be
the season of the witch - look:
dark clouds dream the rain..."

". . . violet morning
and the gallop of dry leaves:
time is a turtle. . ."

"... Baton Rouge's midnight:
an abysmal rouge sky which spits
thunderbolts. I'm cool."

"... lonely days - lonely
friends from live-oaks, I'm crying:
I'll leave you some day. . ."

". . . golden lake at dawn
thrilled by the eagle's high call -
Lord, thanks: I fly alone. . ."

EPiLOGUE:

> "... *over the mute lake*
> *one eagle flies - splinter of...*
> *haiku diamond...*"

(Theophil Magus, Baton Rouge, Louisiana
July, 1999 - July, 2001)

***

THE END